Shani's Shoebox

1
2
3
4
5
6
7

8
9
10
11
12

First published in the UK in 2018 by Green Bean Books
c/o Pen & Sword Books Ltd
47 Church Street, Barnsley, S. Yorkshire, S70 2AS
www.greenbeanbooks.com

Hardback ISBN 978-1-78438-248-3
Paperback ISBN 978-1-78438-417-3

Translated by Noga Applebaum
Designed by Shona Andrew
Edited by Kate Baker and Claire Berliner

Printed in China by 1010 Printing International Ltd

081830K1/B1236/A5

Shani's Shoebox

Written and Illustrated by

Rinat Hoffer

Translated by Noga Applebaum

“I have a present for you,”
Shani’s Aba said.
“Shoes for Rosh Hashanah,
all shiny and red.”

Shani tried them on
and threw the box to the floor.
It was only a box, after all,
nothing more.

An ordinary box that had come from the shop,
with a pale grey lid and a stripe on top.

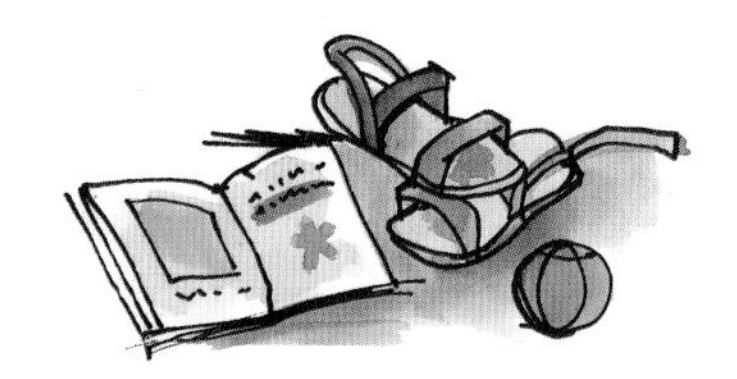

The box lay hidden behind Duck and Bear,
and on Yom Kippur Shani found it there.

She cut out windows and doors, one by one;
glued leaves on the roof and the *sukkah* was done.

She added decorations at school the next day –
seven fruits made from paper,
seven guests made of clay.

But after Sukkot the box was thrown out,
and the strong autumn wind blew it about.
Once again it was only a box from the shop,
with a slightly squashed lid and a stripe on the top.

As winter came a cat passed it by
and mewed to herself, "How lucky am I!"
When the wild wind blew and rain fell to the ground,
the cat was all snug in the bed she had found.

She was still in the box, sleeping tight,
as Hanukkah candles were burning bright.

Hanukkah ended
and the days flew past,
until outside the almond tree
blossomed at last.
There in the yard
lay the box from the shop,
with a slightly damp lid
and some mud on the top.

Tu B'Shvat came, plants sprouted and grew . . .
white daffodils and pink tulips too.
Out of the shoebox a buttercup sprang.
"My box is a flowerpot!" Shani sang.

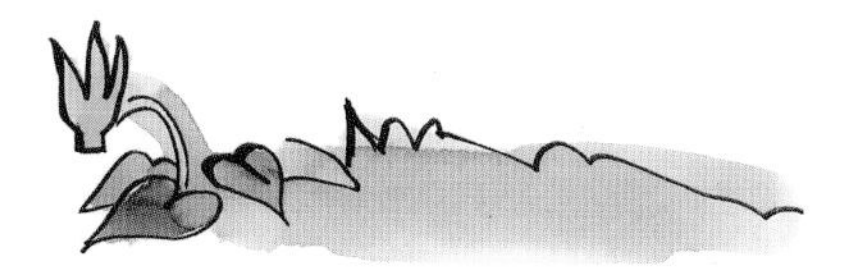

Shani replanted the flower with pride
and left the shoebox forgotten, outside.

There it stayed, that box from the shop,
getting crumpled and dirty,
with cobwebs on top.

Just before Purim, guess what Shani did?
She tied on some string, made a mask from the lid!

Ima filled the box with *hamantaschen* and sweets –
a *mishloach manot* full of festive treats.
In school Ori ate more than his share,
and the box was returned, now empty and bare.

Once more the shoebox was left out of sight,
until the day the sun shone bright.
Turtledoves nested, wing touching wing.
At home spring cleaning was in full swing.

Aba worked hard to make everything clean
so the mess and *chametz* could no longer be seen.
Ima was tidying the house all around,
and things that were lost were suddenly found.

Shani's sister Gal took the box from the shelf
and claimed it as a treasure chest for herself.
She added some glitter
and drew on some paintings,
then filled it with all of her
trinkets and playthings.

The very next day her friends took great pleasure
in emptying out all of the treasure.
And under the bed, the box from the shop
lay there all pink, with
sparkles on top.

Passover arrived, and on Seder night,
the *afikoman* was hidden from sight.

Shani soon found it and claimed her prize
– a new baby doll with sparkling eyes.

She laid her doll in the box, with a smile,
like Moses' reed basket afloat on the Nile.

Yom HaAtzma'ut was drawing near.
Gal said: "I'm hanging the flag this year!"
But she couldn't quite reach, for all that she tried,
so she ran to get the old box from inside.

Ima worried but Aba said it was cool
for Gal to climb on her makeshift stool
and hang the flag triumphantly
for all of Israel (and the neighbours) to see.

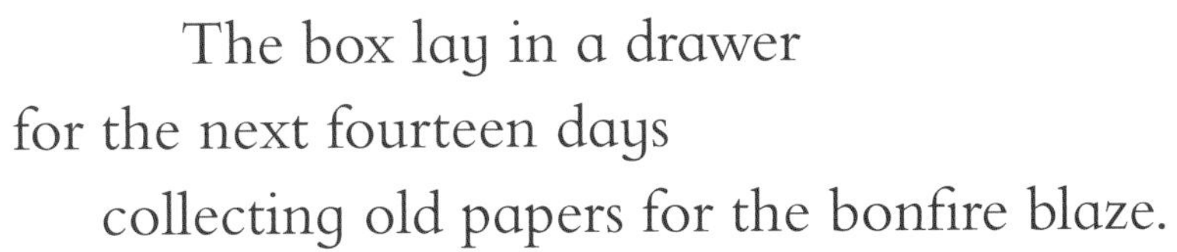

The box lay in a drawer
for the next fourteen days
collecting old papers for the bonfire blaze.

On Lag B'Omer the box held a stash
of warm baked potatoes all covered in ash.

Ima fixed the box, and look what she made –
a beautiful basket for the Shavuot parade.
Full of fresh fruit it was sure to impress
– the same goes for Shani
in her new white dress.

Two grapes were all
that were left from the crop;
Ima cleaned the box
and cut a slot in the top.
"Surprise! I made us
a polling station.
We all get to vote where
to go on vacation!"

"Summer holidays are drawing near,
so write your requests and put them
in here."

Aba wrote "Africa", Shani chose "space".
Gal drew on her note a pink horsey place!

Ima counted the votes and said with glee,
"We're off to Eilat, to swim in the sea!"
While the girls played with sand
on the beach,
the box was left on a shelf,
out of reach.

The summer was over, and just as before,
a new year was knocking at Shani's door.

Again Aba said, "A present for you!
A new pair of shoes, and this time they're blue.
There's a dash of yellow and a dash of pink
. . . for Rosh Hashanah – what do you think?"

That's funny, Shani suddenly thought,
the shoes are new, but the box? It is not!

The very same box, so old but so dear,
brought memories back of the previous year.
Shani lifted the lid, peered in and smiled
as her imagination began to run wild . . .

Through the whole year, Shani's mind was zooming.
She saw *dreidels*, a *sukkah*, the almond tree blooming.
A clown picking *hamantaschen*, hung up high;
matzah kites flying away in the sky.
Flags and bonfires; sunflowers standing tall.
Winter to spring, then summer, then fall . . .

Shana
Tova

One year is over, there's a new one ahead.
And Shani? Shhh . . . she's sound asleep in her bed.

Rosh Hashanah
1
Shana Tova
Honey
Yom Kippur
2
Sukkot
3
AUTUMN
Hanukkah
4
Tu B'Shvat
5
WINTER

Purim
6
Passover
7
SPRING
HAGGADAH
SUMMER
Lag B'Omer
9
8
Yom HaAtzma'ut
10
Shavuot